LOST

by Paul Brett Johnson
and Celeste Lewis

Illustrated by
Paul Brett Johnson

Orchard Books / New York

NOTE: Flag was a real dog. He was lost in the harsh desert of Tonto National Forest north of Cave Creek, Arizona. For four weeks we tried to find him. We can only imagine Flag's story, the fierce odds he must have faced in his struggle to survive.—C.L.

Orchard Books, 95 Madison Avenue, New York, NY 10016
Manufactured in the United States of America. Printed by Barton Press, Inc. Bound by Horowitz/Rae. Book design by Mina Greenstein.
The text of this book is set in 16 point Photina. The illustrations are acrylic and colored pencil reproduced in full color.
10 9 8 7 6 5 4 3 2

Library of Congress Cataloging-in-Publication Data.
Johnson, Paul Brett. Lost / by Paul Brett Johnson and Celeste Lewis ; illustrated by Paul Brett Johnson.   p.   cm.   "A Richard Jackson book"—
Half t.p.   Summary: Because she never gives up hope that her beagle, lost in the desert, will be found, the young master keeps
something special in her pocket for her dog.   ISBN 0-531-09501-0.   ISBN 0-531-08851-0 (lib. bdg.)
[1. Dogs—Fiction. 2. Lost and found possessions—Fiction. 3. Deserts—Fiction.] I. Lewis, Celeste. II. Title.
PZ7.J6354Lo 1995 [E]—dc20 95-20846

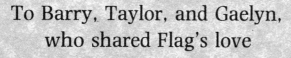

To Barry, Taylor, and Gaelyn,
who shared Flag's love

—C.L.

Remembering Toby

—P.B.J.

The day Flag got lost in the desert,
Dad and I searched for him till sundown.

We found some dog tracks at a watering hole
and some other tracks too—big scary ones.

But we didn't find Flag.

Monday morning I made a lost-dog poster.
It said, *REWARD: $8.48*. That's how much I had
in my piggy bank. I hoped it would be enough.

Dad took my poster to work and made copies.
After school we drove out into the desert again,
tacking them up along the way.

Finally, three days later, someone called.
A lady had found a lost beagle. I couldn't wait
till we got to her house. Flag was going to be
so happy.

But it wasn't Flag.
I sat beside the strange dog and stroked his head.
I gave him the biscuit I had brought.

Before bed I got out my photos of Flag. I couldn't
help crying. But I laughed some too.

The picture of Flag catching lima beans
was my favorite. That was Flag's best trick.
I hate lima beans, so Flag got mine.
Every time I threw one in the air,
he would catch it.
Once he caught sixteen in a row!

The next day Dad came home with a big map. It had a million squiggly lines that showed every ridge and gully.

Dad thought Cave Creek Canyon would be a good place to look for Flag.

The canyon was rough going. We had to crawl on all fours over huge rocks and through prickly underbrush.

Suddenly there was a howl that sounded
just like Flag. We started yelling his name.
"Flag! Flag!"
We kept on calling and listening.
But all we heard was our own voices
echoing back at us.

At school I couldn't concentrate, even though
we were studying astronomy, which I really like.
There was a big cactus just outside the window.
It made me think of the desert.
And Flag.
Where was he?

I missed him so much.

Friday came at last. Dad had promised
we could look for Flag again.
But the whole weekend turned out to be
a big fat zero. All we saw was a pack of javelinas.
Dad said they could be mean, so we steered clear.

I hated the desert!

Next time out we climbed a fire tower. I knew
Flag was somewhere below, looking for me
just as hard as I was looking for him.
But where?
There was so much ground still to cover.
Please, Flag. Don't give up!

Later we met an old prospector. He said
he once had a dog that got lost in the desert,
but he never found him. He said it didn't
look good for Flag.
I told him if any dog could make it, Flag could.

We gave him our address and phone number,
just in case.

Friday night there was a knock on my door.
Dad came into the room and sat beside me
on the bed. He took my hand.
He said we had to talk.

I knew then we wouldn't be packing up
and heading out to the desert anymore.
Flag had been lost almost a month.

Dad? Please?
Flag's still out there.
Waiting for us to come find him.
I know he is.

At breakfast Dad said maybe we should go
to the animal shelter and look for another beagle.
But I didn't want another beagle. I wanted Flag.
Dad was just trying to cheer us both up, I guess.

I marked another X on the calendar. I hoped Flag
didn't think I had forgotten him.

Monday when I got home from school,
there was a truck in the driveway. I recognized
the old man we had met in the desert.

I began to run.

Flag was all scratched up, and he was down
to skin and bones. I hated to think what he must have
gone through. He was bad off, the prospector said,
but he would be fine.

When I took Flag in my arms,
he wriggled a little
and tried to lick my face.

I reached in my pocket
and showed him what I had
been keeping—a dried lima bean.

"For good luck," I whispered.
"I never gave up hope."